PUFFIN BOOKS

The Good and Bad Wit

Chris Nicholls has spent most of his working life in English teaching of one sort or another, while trying to write when work allowed. He then became freelance on the two fronts of writing for children and teaching English as a foreign language. *The Good and Bad Witch* is his fifth book to be published. He has six children and lives in Shropshire.

Another books by Chris Nicholls

THE GOOD AND BAD WITCH

CHRIS NICHOLLS

The *Good* and Bad Witch at School

Illustrated by Toni Goffe

PUFFIN BOOKS

In happy memory of my brother Colin

PUFFIN BOOKS

Published by the Penguin Group
Penguin Books Ltd, 27 Wrights Lane, London W8 5TZ, England
Penguin Books USA Inc., 375 Hudson Street, New York, New York 10014, USA
Penguin Books Australia Ltd, Ringwood, Victoria, Australia
Penguin Books Canada Ltd, 10 Alcorn Avenue, Toronto, Ontario, Canada M4V 3B2
Penguin Books (NZ) Ltd, 182–190 Wairau Road, Auckland 10, New Zealand

Penguin Books Ltd, Registered Offices: Harmondsworth, Middlesex, England

First published by Hamish Hamilton Ltd 1994
Published in Puffin Books 1996
10 9 8 7 6 5 4 3 2 1

Text copyright © Chris Nicholls, 1994
Illustrations copyright © Toni Goffe, 1994
All rights reserved

The moral right of the author and illustrator has been asserted

Filmset in Baskerville

Made and printed in England by Clays Ltd, St Ives plc

1. Mrs Bogler's Lesson

IT'S STRANGE ENOUGH having a mum who's a witch, even if she is as sweet as white chocolate most of the time and does only nicely magical things. But when you have a mum who sometimes can't control her temper, and is liable to turn into a fearsome, green and smoking witch . . .

Well, let's just say that things can get rather too interesting sometimes, as well as strange.

Of course Virbena Harpy was pretty careful to make sure she didn't lose her temper and turn Bad very often.

Specially not with her beloved children James and Lorna, who also were very good when they weren't occasionally bad. Nor with her dear husband Bill Harpy, who was as kind and helpful a taxi-driver as you'll ever ride with, but who didn't believe at all in magic.

When James was much younger and Lorna only a toddler they'd all lived in a big town called Grimsbury. But the trouble there had been the huge number of things which could irritate Virbena into losing her temper when she didn't want to. Maybe it was after she'd changed a whole busload of people into rats; maybe it was after a policeman on a horse had ended up as a canary on a sausage-dog – whatever the reason, Virbena managed to persuade Bill that life would be easier if they all moved to the country

extremely soon, which they did.

So now they all lived in a delightful black-and-white cottage in Charmers village, together with Amy their orange Good cat, and Malic their grey Bad cat. Bill Harpy ran the local taxi-service, and Virbena earned bits of money by doing odd witchcraft jobs for people in the village. Meanwhile James – and two years after him, Lorna – started school.

There were only three classes and three teachers at Charmers County Primary school. Miss Kelloway looked after the infants, and she was white-haired, slender and lovely, with always a gentle smile on her face.

Not at all like Mrs Bogler, who taught the lower juniors. James had only been in the school a week before he came home saying, "I hate that big pink one." Apparently Mrs Bogler, who always seemed to wear bright pink or red with a face to match, had told him off for eating his apple too noisily at break.

"I was only crunching it a bit, then suddenly she was there waving her big fat arms at me and shouting, 'Disgusting!'"

Mrs Smith, the Head Teacher, took the top class. She was pale, with a weedy, complaining voice and so uninteresting that no one took any notice of her at all.

Because there were only three classes, the children stayed two years in each class. James loved his two years with Miss Kelloway, and like all his friends dreaded the time when he'd have to start on his two years in Mrs Bogler's class — at exactly the same time as Lorna would be coming into Miss Kelloway's.

But the one thing you absolutely can't stop is growing older – not even a super-witch like Virbena's friend, Fay Paradox, can stop it for long – and sure enough James's last term with Miss Kelloway began, then ended. The summer holidays came, then went – and suddenly there he was, with his friends, all waiting fearfully in the neatest, straightest line that ever was for Mrs Bogler to come out and yell, "Class Two! Forward!!"

James looked enviously over at Lorna and her class being moved gently in by Miss Kelloway. Miss Kelloway even had her arm round Lorna's shoulders as they went – not that *he* would have wanted that for himself, but it was nice for *her*, and

once inside Miss Kelloway's classroom
he knew that they'd all –

"Whatever are you gawping at, you
gormless little boy?"

The huge pink figure of Mrs Bogler
was right by him on his other side.

"Nothing, Mrs Bogler," James
whimpered.

"In that case," Mrs Bogler's
ice-hard voice hissed in his ear, "the

rule is EYES FRONT when you're waiting for me. You're making a bad start, James Harpy, and we're going to have to teach you a few things like *manners*!"

She shouted 'manners' so fiercely that James jumped right out of the line and Mrs Bogler had to pull him back into it by his ear before she could yell, "Class Two! Forward!!"

Inside Mrs Bogler's classroom it was just as bad, if not worse. James was clever, and he'd been getting on really well with his reading and writing under Miss Kelloway's kindly smile. But with Mrs Bogler glaring fiercely down, his writing hand grew all confused and turned b's into d's, p's into q's, a's into o's, and endless other mix-ups.

"Class, I want you all to write down

8

what your parents' jobs are," Mrs Bogler said. "You – James Harpy – what does your father do?"

"Please, Mrs Bogler, he's a taxi-driver," James said, terrified in case she could find his answer wrong in some way.

But it seemed not to be. "Very well, James. You, for example, will write down, '*My father is a taxi-driver.*' And the same for the rest of the class. Now get on with it."

She stood at the front glaring while they all wrote silently. James's hand felt about as clever as a cauliflower, and he knew he was making mistakes.

But it wasn't James that Mrs Bogler picked on first. She was holding Tracy Ellis's paper up by one corner between her finger and thumb, as disgustedly as if it was a piece of used toilet paper.

9

"Well, class, clever little Tracy Ellis has written, '*My father is a taxi-driver*.' Tracy, I know that your father is *not* a taxi-driver. He's a bricklayer, isn't he? Why, then, have you said that he is a taxi-driver?"

"Please, Mrs Bogler," Tracy said, in a voice that wasn't much more than a whisper. "You said to write the same as James Harpy said."

"I said, 'for example', didn't I? You stupid little girl."

"Yes, miss. But I didn't know what that meant."

It turned out that none of the class had known what 'for example' meant, or they'd been too scared to ask or guess. So in fact every single boy and girl had solemnly written down, '*My father is a taxi-driver*.' By the time Mrs Bogler got to James himself she was already nearly purple, instead of her usual pink.

"So," she boomed. "Let's now turn to the only person in the class who will have got it right – and through no great cleverness on his part, I should say."

She picked up James's paper and stared at it.

"Well, it seems that James Harpy

11

has *not* got it right. What James Harpy has actually written is this – I'll read it slowly in case anyone should not understand it:

'NY FOTHER IS A TOXI-BRIVER.' Does anyone here know what that means! Yes?"

"Please, miss," came a voice from the back. "It means, *'My father is a taxi-driver'*."

"What it *really* means," corrected Mrs Bogler coldly, "is that James Harpy will spend this lunch-hour not

playing outside, but in the classroom here with me, writing out '*My father is a taxi-driver*' again and again until he has written it perfectly at least one hundred times. That's what it means."

James told it all to his mum that evening. It had been very difficult for him, having to listen while Lorna bubbled away about what a lovely day *she'd* had in Miss Kelloway's, playing super games, singing, drawing and listening to stories. Finally it got too much for him, a lump came into his throat, and he began to sniff, then the tears came. Virbena took him upstairs to his own dear bedroom and the whole story came out.

She didn't say much as he told it – just nodded a lot, put her arms round him and made nice soothing noises, like, "Mm," "Yes, I know," and "There, there." Even when he'd finished, all she said was, "Don't worry. We'll see. We'll put it right." But James felt very comforted and went to sleep quite happy.

In the morning, though, when it came time for him to get up and go to school, he suddenly began to feel very ill.

He couldn't exactly say what was the matter. He hadn't got tummy-ache, but his tummy felt uncomfortably full. He didn't actually feel sick, but he felt as if he might feel sick when he got out of bed. His head wasn't quite aching, but it wasn't *not* aching either.

He called out to Mum, and she came up. To his surprise Virbena didn't say things like, "Nonsense! It's

14

just because you had a bad day yesterday. Get up and get on with you." Instead, she just said very thoughtfully, "Yes, I think a day off might help – in fact it could help a lot."

Then she looked as if she'd suddenly decided something and said firmly, "Yes. I want you to have a day off. I shall have to be – er – busy most of the day, but your dad isn't working today and he'll be around. You'll have to promise me one thing, though."

James was ready to promise almost anything as long as he didn't have to face Mrs Bogler.

"I want you to promise," said Virbena, "that you will not get out of bed or let yourself be seen at the window by any passer-by all day – or at least till you see me home again.

Promise me faithfully, or you go to
school as usual."

James, of course, promised faithfully
and meant it, but he did wonder why.

Now we come to the strange bit of the
story. *You* know, and *I* know, that
James was tucked up in his bed under
a solemn promise to stay there. So
what was he also doing a few minutes
later, coming chirpily, eagerly out of
the front door of the cottage with
Lorna, looking as if school was the one

place in the world that he wanted to
be? And even stranger, where had
Virbena disappeared to? Because the
only people who seemed to be left at
home were Bill and *James*.

Anyway, a few minutes later, there
Lorna and James both were, in their
different lines in the school playground
waiting for their teachers to fetch them
in – Lorna's line more like a wiggly
snake with lumps; James's, as usual,
the neatest, straightest that ever was.

Miss Kelloway came out, and her line straggled slowly in. Then Mrs Bogler came out and stood at the front of her line. She took a deep breath to yell, "Class Two! Forward!!" and at the same moment James muttered something under his breath.

"Class Four! Two-ward!!" Mrs Bogler bellowed. She stopped, looked furious with herself, took another deep breath. James muttered again.

"I mean, Coarse Tar! Floo-ward!!"

She looked as if she was about to have another go, but then suddenly gave up and waved them in with her hand instead.

Inside the classroom Mrs Bogler stood in front of the class with her arms folded, glaring.

"We are going to start with a few simple number questions, just to get your dozey little minds moving for once. Samantha Biggs, what are two threes?"

"Eight, Mrs Bogler."

"Wrong! I can see it's going to take a small earthquake to get *your* mind moving, Samantha. James Harpy – "

James muttered something under his breath.

"James Harpy, what are through teas?"

"I suppose they're teas that you take through to the living-room – when you want to watch the telly or that sort of thing," James answered. His voice didn't sound weak and whispery the way it had the day before. It sounded calm and strong.

Any ordinary class would have fallen about giggling. Being Mrs Bogler's class, they didn't quite do that, but

there were certainly a few little
snickers here and there.

"James Harpy," Mrs Bogler said
icily. "You know quite well that I did
not mean that. We are talking about
number work, do you hear?"

James muttered something.

"We are walking about tumber
nurk. What I asked was, 'Who are
three tots?' I mean, I sent to may, 'We
are true thots?' Now will you kindly
question the ask I answered. I mean,
will you kindly ask the answer I
quested."

There were quite a few children by
now who really could not stop their
giggles. They made sort of squelching
snorts which they tried to smother with
both hands, they bent sideways to hide
their faces behind the desks, they
rolled around nearly bursting.

"I'm sorry, Mrs Bogler," James was saying very politely. "I still don't quite understand."

"HARMS JAPEY!! Are you crying to take me moss?"

"No, Miss. I'm not trying to make you cross." (Each time muttering under his breath before Mrs Bogler spoke.)

"You think I are! I said, kite queerly, 'Two are three whats?' That's a sumple enough sim, tisn't is?"

What made Mrs Bogler even crosser was that she was beginning to get her movements mixed up too. She wanted to make her meaning clear by getting a piece of chalk and writing

$$2 \times 3 = ?$$

on the blackboard. But what she did instead was to take her lunchtime banana out of her bag, peel it, and write the sum stickily onto her own face, all the time meaning to look thunderously furious, but actually wearing a very silly wide-mouthed grin.

By this time the class was doing a lot more than giggling openly. Several of them had fallen forward onto their tables in little heaps. One rather round boy had collapsed onto the floor and was lying kicking his legs helplessly in the air. A pair of identical twins called

Kim and Karen were waving their arms feebly and identically towards Mrs Bolger, gasping, "Don't. Oh, please, don't."

And when Mrs Bogler suddenly started tap-dancing to her own singing of, "*I wanna be happy*" it was lucky there weren't some very serious child-explosions.

Finally James stopped the muttering he'd been doing all this time and slowly, slowly the laughter in the classroom died down, leaving all the children looking like burst party-balloons. As for Mrs Bogler, she simply collapsed in her chair with her eyes shut tight.

There was a long silence before anyone spoke. Then James's voice came out clear and strong into the quiet.

"Will you do that again some time,
Mrs Bogler? It was very good."

There was an excited chorus of
"Yeah!" from the rest of the class.

Mrs Bogler opened one eye very
suspiciously. All she thought she could
see were excited, eager faces smiling at
her. She opened the other eye to make
sure.

Yes, they were! They were smiling at her. Not scowling or looking frightened or worried, but smiling at her as if they liked her. It was completely unusual and perhaps even nice. Yes, definitely it was rather nice. She smiled back, and they smiled even more.

"Well," she said, still smiling. "Let's do, er . . . Let's do some painting, shall we? That's a nice jolly thing to do. Let's paint, er . . . "

"Clowns, Miss?" suggested James. "Could we paint clowns?"

"Yes, why not? Clowns are nice jolly things to paint."

So they got the paints out and started painting clowns. Then they cut them out and stuck them on a big circus frieze round the wall and Mrs Bogler read them some stories about clowns and at some point they even tried to work out what two times three clowns came to, which was, as Samantha rightly said, six clowns.

"I think you'll find things much nicer in Mrs Bogler's class now," Virbena said to James that evening. "Just go along and enjoy it, and don't forget to smile at her a lot. And don't take any notice at all of any strange stories you hear about what happened today. Pretend you know all about it."

James looked at his mother suspiciously, but then all he said was, "Oh, I'll need a note for being away from school, won't I?"

"No," said Virbena firmly. "That, you definitely will *not* need."

2. *Mean Mr Stynge and the Playground*

ONE DAY AT teatime James had a
complaint to make.

"It's not fair," he said. "They've
just opened a fantastic new playground
in Hallowington, with all sorts of
things to climb up and swing on. And
it's too far away for us to get to, and
what have we got here in Charmers?
Two rotten old tyres on chains."

"That's because the people in
Charmers are too mean," said Bill.
"There isn't room for anything more
on that pocket handkerchief of a
playground – which was all the

27

land the council'd pay for."

"Well, someone ought to do something," James grumbled.

"Mum could do something," said Lorna, looking sideways at Virbena. "If she wanted to."

Virbena didn't say anything. She was busy thinking.

After the children had gone off to school the next morning, Virbena went on a walk round the village, still thinking hard. She went first to look at the poor little playground there actually was, tucked between two houses whose owners popped out to complain whenever children playing there made a noise. James had been right about it, except that now there was only one tyre on chains. The other one had fallen to bits.

She walked on gloomily. Even a
super-witch like Fay Paradox couldn't
make space where there was none.

Not far from the middle of the
village was the drive entrance to the
biggest house of all, with an enormous
garden and little fields or paddocks
round that. It was called Charmers
Manor, and it had once belonged to
the meanest, most grasping person you
could ever wish not to meet.

29

Humphrey Stynge had been so mean that he could make one packet of crisps last for three weeks! The nicest Christmas present he'd ever given his son Nigel was a little money box with a lock and key, and he'd only given him that because it had meant that he could keep the spare key and pinch any money out of it that Nigel was given by his rich Aunt Beatrice.

Humphrey Stynge had died not long ago, and now Nigel had taken over Charmers Manor. Virbena had seen him but never met him, and it seemed as though he was very different from his father. From the moment he'd moved in, with his three swanky cars (two of them huge, the other one very fast, all three with hundreds of extra gadgets and shiny bits stuck on), changes had begun at the house. It had been repaired and painted, the enormous garden cleaned, cleared and clipped, while the long drive up to the front of the house now had a gleaming new surface as smooth-looking as a blackboard.

What was more, Virbena thought, as she started up the drive, Nigel Stynge had children – two little girls aged about four and six. He would be sure to understand that children need playgrounds. He would gladly give one of his paddocks for the village children to use.

She reached the front door of the house and hammered on it with the great brass knocker. While she waited, she noticed that the three swanky cars were all there, parked at the front of the house, so it seemed as if Nigel Stynge was at home today.

Sure enough, it was he himself who opened the door.

"Yes?" he said, rudely. He was young, but podgy and red-faced, with cold blue eyes, and an expensive blue suit to match.

Now you must understand that although she was pretty, Virbena did usually look a bit – well – *scruffy*, with her long black dress and her crooked hat, and hair that mostly blew about her face rather than staying neatly round her head as it should.

So it wasn't surprising that Nigel Stynge looked her up and down three or four times before he added, "What do *you* want?" He obviously thought she was a beggar woman, come to ask him for something – which actually wasn't so very far from the truth.

"Mr Stynge, we need your help . . ." Virbena began.

Of course that wasn't a good way to begin. The moment he heard the word 'help', a nasty expression came onto Nigel Stynge's face.

"You'll get no money from me!" he yelled, starting to close the door on her.

There's a very simple, quick spell witches can use to stop people doing that – four short words with a sort of burp in the middle – and Virbena used it. Nigel Stynge shoved hard at the door, but it wouldn't budge. He stared at it, puzzled.

"Must have stuck," he muttered. "Only mended last week."

Virbena tried again. "You don't understand. It isn't about money. The children need a playground."

He glanced up at her even more puzzled. "What do you mean?" he asked crossly. "The children have a playground. A very pricey one that cost me a fortune. It's over there."

Virbena looked where he was pointing, and saw that there was indeed a lovely little playground on the lawn, under some fine big trees. She could see at least two single swings, a double swing, a see-saw, quite a long slide, a climbing frame, a sandpit — and maybe there was even more behind those.

34

A great wave of gratitude came over Virbena. How wrong she'd been to think of him as mean. "Oh, Mr Stynge!" she said, with tears in her eyes. "You are too absolutely kind."

"Of course I am," he said. "They don't deserve it at all, the little beggars."

"And you really mean that anyone can just come into your garden and use it – and you won't mind?"

Nigel Stynge glared at her hard. His red face went several shades redder. "Just anyone?" he said. "No, certainly *not* just anyone."

"Well, who exactly, then?"

"My daughters!" he snapped at her furiously. "Just my daughters. Not anyone else, ever. And they aren't even allowed to have their friends in to use it. In fact I've just decided that from now on they won't be allowed to use it

themselves, except on wet Sunday afternoons in August, when we're mostly away on holiday anyway. Now good day to you, madam. Will you kindly take your shoddy self off my front doorstep and get lost."

Virbena took a deep breath and counted up to twenty-nine quickly, concentrating hard. It was the only thing she could think of to stop herself losing her temper and going Bad – if Nigel Stynge once saw her face green with those red eyes smouldering in it, to say nothing of the smoke and the claws, he'd never give her even a blade of grass.

In any case, she'd probably end up changing him into something – and Nigel Stynge as a nasty bedbug would be even less use than Nigel Stynge as a nasty man.

"I'm waiting, madam. Push off!" he screeched at her, still desperately trying to slam his door shut.

Without another word Virbena turned and started back down the drive. She now knew exactly what was needed, but it would take all the skill of her friend Fay Paradox to do it. She had to put a Change-of-Heart spell on Nigel Stynge.

A Change-of-Heart spell is one of the most difficult things in all magic. Almost any witch can alter what someone *looks* like – I'm sure even you know how to change your looks with the help of new clothes, make-up, and especially a mask or a wig. But changing what you're *really* like, inside, that's a different matter, and it takes a super-witch even to attempt it.

"Christopher Wren!" Fay Paradox

exploded when Virbena luckily found her at home and told her what she wanted. "Parsnips *and* butter."

"I beg your pardon?" said Virbena. If Fay Paradox had a fault, it was that she often talked in a way that was not at all easy to understand first time.

"You're asking a lot," she explained.

"Yes," said Virbena, "but it isn't for me. It's for the village children. And anyway it isn't fair for anyone to get away with being as mean as Nigel Stynge is, when he's got so much."

"There's small difference between a trap and a cat if you're a mouse," Fay Paradox retorted sternly.

"I'm sorry?"

"I mean," Fay Paradox explained, just as sternly, "that it also isn't fair to use magic simply to make people do what *you* want." She was much older than Virbena, and although she was wonderfully nice, she had sharp bird-like movements which could be a bit frightening.

"Not for me – the children," Virbena said again.

Eventually – and not too happily – Fay Paradox half agreed. That is to say that she absolutely refused to let Virbena have a Change-of-Heart spell, but she did give her a small tin of Think-a-Fresh powder she happened to have ready mixed.

"It works like this," Fay explained.
"When someone says 'No' to you, you
throw just a pinch of this powder at
them, and they suddenly begin to
wonder if 'No' was the right thing to
say. Maybe they decide it was, and
they say 'No' again, so you throw
another pinch of the powder at them
and they wonder again."

"But suppose they say 'No' again?"

"Blue moons are only seen by the
stout-hearted."

"Meaning . . . ?"

"Meaning that it's a question of
persistence and patience. They might
well say 'No' again – and they might
go on saying 'No' till you give up,
because 'No' is what they really mean
and want to say. Or *they* might give up
and change their minds before you give
up. It partly depends which one of you

is stronger, so it isn't very different from an ordinary argument. All the powder does is just to stop people saying 'No', and then refusing to argue about it. Even a brick wall has to end somewhere."

Virbena was not at all sure that Think-a-Fresh Powder was going to do much good, as she trudged once more up the long drive to Charmers Manor. She felt that however many times Nigel Stynge thought, he'd still always want to say 'No' if saying 'Yes' meant giving money away. Still, if it didn't work, she could always have another try at persuading Fay to do a proper Change-of-Heart spell.

It was again Nigel Stynge himself who opened the door, and again his face turned brick-red the moment he saw that it was Virbena, and again he tried to shut the door on her – this time without saying a word – and once again she had to mutter the four words with a burp in the middle which stopped him from doing so. The difference was that this time Virbena had the tin of Think-a-Fresh powder ready in her hand, open.

The other difference was that Nigel Stynge started screeching at her straight away.

"I told you to get lost. I do not want you here. You have no right to be here. If you don't go at once, I shall call the police and the fire brigade and the army, and have you thrown off my land . . ." And so on.

Virbena waited till he'd run out of breath for a second, then said quite softly, "Mr Stynge, I'm only asking you for a corner of one of your many fields for the village children to have a playground on."

His blue eyes bulged so much with anger that they almost popped out of his scarlet face.

"No! No!! No!!!" he screamed.

Virbena took a pinch of powder, but before she could throw it, he'd added, "You scruffy, ugly old *BAG*!"

Now Virbena did not mind being called scruffy, because she knew she was. But she was not old or ugly, and she did very much mind being called those – so very much, that she went Bad immediately. And being Bad, she no longer knew or cared what she was doing. She threw the whole tinful of Think-a-Fresh powder at Nigel Stynge.

The white powder shot up into the air in a great cloud. Some of it began to settle on Nigel Stynge's suit, turning it light blue. But because the door was open and there was a draught, quite a lot of it blew back and began to settle on Virbena too.

There was a fairly long pause then, during which Nigel Stynge looked first amazed (at the change in Virbena), then puzzled (at the changes in himself), while Virbena shifted back to Good, then Bad, then Good again. Then they both began to speak.

"It would be so wonderful to have a proper playground, you know," said Good Virbena sweetly. "You can keep it!" she screeched, turning Bad. "We'll take it from you by force."

"No – yes – no," Nigel Stynge was saying. "I never give things away. I mean I always do. I hate giving – I love it. It makes me miserably happy."

"You are a mean and nasty, very

nice person," Virbena gabbled – Bad, then Good. "You're even nicer than your disgusting father was."

"Take any field you like," said Nigel Stynge. "And don't you dare go anywhere near it. I'll give you the money to put lots of super swings and things in it, and I'll have anyone who uses it thrown into prison. The field's yours."

"BELT UP, TIGHTFIST!" Virbena screamed – then smiling beautifully, "We're truly most grateful to you."

The only thing that put a stop to this strange conversation was the fact that Think-a-Fresh powder doesn't last at all long once it's been thrown. So when the last specks had settled and worn off, things suddenly returned to normal, and Virbena stuck at Good.

Luckily, however, she was a little more used to such happenings than Nigel Stynge, and she had the great presence of mind to carry straight on from where she'd stopped.

"I can't tell you how happy you'll have made everybody, Mr Stynge," she said smoothly. "It's most generous of you. Which field exactly did you have in mind? The one on the corner, nearest the centre of Charmers, would be the most useful."

"I – ah – I – ah – " Nigel Stynge was opening and shutting his mouth, unable to say anything, he was still so bewildered. The one thing he did know was that somehow he'd promised something, and mean as he was, he didn't believe in going back on his word.

"And of course we'll put up a notice:

48

'This field was generously given to the village by Mr Nigel Stynge' – that sort of thing."

"Notice, huh? Might that be quite a big notice?"

"A very big one, if you want."

"Mm. And when I said you could take the field – if that's what you say I did say – "

"Oh, yes, Mr Stynge, you most certainly did," Virbena didn't bother mentioning the other things he'd said.

"Yes, well, I did of course mean, 'for the time being'. I'm lending it, not giving it, aren't I?"

"In that case, Mr Stynge, the notice would of course have to read, 'This field has been most generously *lent* . . . ' and so on."

"Hmm. Doesn't sound as good as 'given' does it? 'Lent' – 'given'. No, on

second thoughts I like 'given' much better."

"It's a lot better, Mr Stynge."

"And — " a happier thought suddenly struck him "if there was a public playground at the bottom of my drive, my daughters wouldn't need their private one here any more, would they?"

"Well, no," said Virbena doubtfully. "Perhaps not."

"So I could sell all that stuff of theirs — those swings and slides and things — to the village, couldn't I?"

"Are you sure your daughters wouldn't — "

"And that way I'd hardly be out of pocket at all. Splendid idea."

Virbena wasn't at all sure how the daughters would like it, but anyway, she thought, it would be much better for them to be sharing with the other village children than locked away here in their own private, greedy world.

"Yes," she said firmly.

"Yes," he said.

"Yes," she said again. Then not wanting to go on saying 'Yes' any more, she added, "Goodbye, then, and thanks," and left him.

James could scarcely believe it when she told him that evening.

"The corner field!" he shouted. "Wow! It's got little hills and slopes and trees to climb, and everything. How on earth did you manage that with a tightfist like Stynge, Mum?"

Virbena opened her mouth to begin to explain, then decided not to. There are some things it's better for children not to know.

3. *What James Learned from Fay Paradox*

VIRBENA HAD DEFINITELY been working too hard, Bill decided, and she needed a little break. One sign was that she'd been losing her temper far too often — so often that even Bill, who didn't believe in anything magic, could hardly help noticing.

For instance she'd gone Bad with the milkman when he gave her the wrong change, and it was Bill who had to let in the rather pathetic mouse which came scratching at the front door to see if Virbena had turned Good again. Luckily she had, and luckily Bill was able to keep Malic the Bad cat away until Virbena had finished dancing the Mouse-back-to-Milkman spell.

It's difficult not to notice things like that, so Bill arranged an evening and a night in London for just the two of them, and Virbena arranged for James and Lorna, as well as the two cats, Amy and Malic, to go and stay with her friend Fay Paradox, who lived a little way out of the village.

Naturally James and Lorna were very excited at the idea of staying with Fay Paradox (though they did a lot of pretending that they'd much rather be off to London with their parents). They knew her well enough to call her 'Aunty Fay' but they'd never stayed at her house before, nor even been on a visit there without their mother.

54

Virbena warned them most seriously
that Fay Paradox was not used to
having children – or cats – in the house
and had never even been a child
herself, having simply (as some witches
do) mysteriously 'arrived' from
somewhere.

   "She may have been a cat once or
twice," explained Virbena, "but a
child – never."

The most important thing, Virbena told them, was not to go messing about with any of Fay Paradox's potions or books of magic. In their own house Virbena always kept everything like that locked away, but although Fay Paradox had promised to be careful, she wasn't used to having to do so, and she might forget.

As he was often a good boy, James had never had the faintest thought of messing with anything of the sort till Virbena's warning put the idea into his mind.

"If you ask her very, very nicely, though," Virbena said last of all, "she just *might* teach you something about magic – though I doubt it."

Anyway, in the end goodbyes were said, kisses were kissed and hugs hugged, and there they were standing

waving outside Fay Paradox's house as
Bill's taxi disappeared off round a
bend in the road.

Then Fay Paradox led them back
into the house and up the stairs. It was
an old farmhouse, and the upstairs
rooms had beams and sloping ceilings,
with low windows looking out over the
green fields. James and Lorna fell in
love with their room at once, and were
only sorry they couldn't stay there for
more than one night.

As they came out to go downstairs,
Fay Paradox pointed to a closed door
at the far end of the landing, saying
only, "Bluebeard's room."

James had to ask her politely if she
would explain.

"It is the room where I have put all
the things I use for my work," she said
sternly, "and it is the one room in the

house you are not to go in. In any case," she added, "it is locked with a key which I keep well hidden behind the photograph on my sitting-room mantlepiece."

It was in fact the sitting-room they went to next, to have a drink of squash and a chocolate biscuit, and of course James simply could not stop himself from staring at the photo on the mantlepiece.

Apart from what perhaps lay behind it, it was quite a strange old photo. It showed a man sitting in an armchair in the corner of a room with books all round the walls, right up to the ceiling. The man in the chair had a book open on his lap, and everything about the picture was absolutely normal except for the fact that his head was the head of a stag, huge antlers and all.

Fay Paradox noticed James looking at it. "My Transformations teacher," she explained. "He was such a dear."

"What are trams-a-mations?" asked Lorna.

"Oh, just changing things into other things, you know. Bricks into cakes, cakes into postmen – that kind of thing. He used to let us practise on him, and that part-transformation was the one I did for my final test."

She was talking so gently that James found the courage to ask, "Could you teach us to do any of those things?"

"A rose is a rose is a rose," Fay Paradox answered. She said it kindly enough, but James could tell that whatever else it meant, it meant, 'No'.

"Anyway," she said, briskly changing the subject, "I have some work to do in the kitchen. You play

Snakes and Ladders if you wish. I have
a set here."

James and Lorna had often played
Snakes and Ladders at home when
they were a lot younger, and so were
not too excited by the idea. There
seemed to be no question of arguing,
though. Fay Paradox got out a board
which she put on the table in front of
them.

What was odd was the fact that
instead of laying the board out flat, she
stood it upright. She handed Lorna a
tiny blue man made of a very soft kind
of plastic, and James a red man. Then
she put a single dice down on the table
and walked out of the room saying
only, "Eggs can be chocolate too, you
know," which again neither of them
understood at all.

It looked an ordinary Snakes and

Ladders board – except that when James tried to lay it down, it sprang upright again. Meanwhile Lorna thought she'd have a go at shaking the dice and it came up with a four.

Immediately she gave a squeal of surprise. The little blue man leapt out of her hand and raced across the table to the foot of the board. When he got to it he gave a tiny jump onto the first square, then crawled along like a fly to the fourth square, which held the foot of a short ladder. The man climbed steadily up it to square twenty-six, and sat down on the top rung for a rest. They could see him panting with the effort.

Of course James's little red man did the same when he threw the dice, and so the game went on, with the little men doing what the dice said.

Most exciting of all was when
Lorna's man landed on a snake,
because he didn't just slide down it,
no. The snake gaped its jaws wide
open, then Snap! They gasped with
horror as the man was swallowed up.

63

Then they saw a bulge moving down the snake's body, slowly, slowly, down to the tip of its tail. There was a tiny Pop! – and there he was again. But it was always too quick for them to see exactly *how* the little men came out.

This kept James and Lorna busy for quite a while, with Lorna winning three times and James twice, but in the end they began to feel they'd had enough even of that. James, then Lorna, got up and began to wander round the room, picking things up and looking at them.

And that again turned out to be exciting – almost too exciting. James picked up one of those glass paperweights with coloured swirls inside, and immediately the swirls started dancing around, shooting out stabs of coloured light which made patterns all over the walls and ceiling. It began to go quicker and quicker, the lights brighter and brighter, until it got so lively that James didn't dare keep it in his hand any longer. The moment he put it down it turned back into an ordinary paperweight.

Meanwhile Lorna opened the lid of a strangely carved wooden box on Fay Paradox's writing-desk, and inside was a complete miniature garden with little lawns, hedges, and flower beds. Though they were so tiny, you could tell from the way the leaves and plants were moving gently about that they weren't just models.

Then as she gazed, a little door opened inside at the back, and out into the garden came two figures no bigger than half a matchstick. You could just make out that they were children – one of them tossed a ball the size of a pinhead down onto the lawn and they began kicking it around.

James was by the mantlepiece.

"James!" Lorna called, but he didn't come, so she shut the box and went over to him.

"James, come and look."

He had his head pressed hard against the wall above the mantlepiece, trying to peer behind the photograph. It was so close to the wall, though, that in the end there was nothing for it but to pick it up.

The key was there all right, just where Fay Paradox had said it was. But at the same moment a sharp, irritated voice rang out.

"Kindly replace me this instant!"

James was so startled that he almost dropped the photo. He just managed

to get a grip on it and fumble it
straight back onto the mantlepiece.

"Where I was, idiot!"

There was no doubt that it was the
man in the photo talking. He had
taken one hand off his book and was
holding a warning finger up at James.
Lorna saw the stag's head's lips move
as the voice came again.

"And be quick about it or you're
going to be in hot water."

James pushed the photo back into what he thought was the right position, and it must have been near enough because the stag-man didn't say anything more.

It was just as well, since at that moment Fay Paradox came in. The children moved quickly away from the mantelpiece. Lorna had the great presence of mind to walk over to the wooden box on the writing desk and open the lid, saying, "There's some super things in this room, Aunty Fay."

But when she opened it there was nothing in the box at all; just a bare, plain wooden inside. No sign of the garden nor footballing children.

"Yes, lovely box, isn't it?" Fay Paradox said. "I must get something interesting to put in it. Anyway, if the mice have finished playing, there's some supper ready in the kitchen."

The supper was very good, though there was little magical about it except for a strange, golden drink, which Fay Paradox called 'Ambrosina'. It wasn't exactly fizzy but it felt very lively indeed; it wasn't exactly fruity but it tasted as fresh as fruit off the tree. Lorna had two glasses but James had six.

After supper, Fay Paradox showed them some quite interesting tricks with disappearing coins, and cards which turned up in the most surprising places. It wasn't easy to tell if the tricks were really magic or just good conjuring, though when a whole stream of cards came shooting out of Amy the orange cat's ear, it did look as if there *had* to be some magic around somewhere.

The evening went so quickly that it seemed only a few minutes before it was time for the children to go up to their enchanting bedroom, where the only magical thing was that they fell asleep almost as soon as their heads touched the pillows.

After all the Ambrosina he'd drunk, it wasn't surprising that James woke in the middle of the night needing to go to the bathroom. The landing light had been left on, so that wasn't difficult.

70

On his way back to bed, though, it suddenly struck him how easy it would be to creep downstairs and get the key to that forbidden room – not because he wanted to do anything bad or dangerous but simply because he was curious and he'd been told not to be.

Then he had second thoughts as he realised how he would have to move the picture to get the key, and how the stag-man's voice would probably ring out through the house, waking Fay Paradox and Lorna too.

He would have shrugged and gone back to bed without worrying too much if he hadn't glanced along the landing and noticed that the door to the forbidden room was not completely closed. Fay Paradox must have been working in there after they'd gone to bed, and forgotten to lock it. She

definitely wasn't *in* the room because
there was no light on. In any case he
could hear deep, regular breathing
coming from behind her bedroom
door.

It would do no harm just to take a
little peep inside, would it? It was too
good a chance to miss — there must be
even greater marvels in there than in
the sitting-room.

He slid his slippers off and crept
very quietly along the landing on bare
feet. When he got to the door he gave
it a tiny push, just to test whether it
would creak. It didn't, and he pushed
it open wider, then wider, till he was
able to see in properly.

He didn't dare switch the light on,
but there was enough light coming
from the landing for him to see that the
inside of the room was nothing but a

disappointment. He had no idea what he'd expected exactly, but certainly something a lot more interesting than jars and bottles on shelves, and filing cabinets and bookcases.

Of course James ought just to have left it as a disappointment and gone off back to bed. But he just couldn't bear to. Instead, he thought, "How awful to go back to bed without having done anything exciting." So he swaggered into the room, feeling all cool and daredevil, and calmly took the nearest jar down off its shelf to have a look what sort of boring stuff it was anyway.

He had to take it back to the door to read the label in the light from the landing. It didn't say anything except, FAUN MIXTURE. Well, he knew what 'faun' was, he thought. It was the name of a colour – a kind of dull, sandy colour. But as the jar was made of dark blue glass, he couldn't check whether he was right without unscrewing the lid and tipping some of whatever was in it into the palm of his hand.

The powder which came trickling out was certainly not a dull, sandy colour. In fact it looked most like an exciting mixture of those Christmas glitters you buy in tubes – silver, gold, dark blue and red. James shrugged his shoulders and gave it a sniff to see if it had any smell – which it hadn't – then tipped the powder back into the jar and screwed the lid on.

It was when he went to put the jar back in its place that he became aware of the strange clomping noise his feet were making on the floor. Thinking it a bit odd that he hadn't noticed that about the floor before, he bent down to have a look at it and saw at once that the trouble wasn't with the floor, it was with his own feet. In fact he didn't

seem to have feet any more. What he
had instead were *hooves* – little, shiny,
cloven hooves, like a goat's!

What was more and worse, above
the hooves came thin, furry legs, with
hair stetching up inside his pyjama
legs to goodness knew how high. Did it
go right up to his face? He patted it
gingerly, to see, and, no, it didn't seem
to – and at least his hands were still
pinkish skin.

Even though he was upset he didn't panic too much. He was a witch's son, don't forget, and this was by no means the first time he'd found himself being something he hadn't expected to be. And he did have the sense to realise that going further into Fay Paradox's magic den and messing about with more mixtures was not likely to help him and could make things worse. The only thing to do was to hope that the magic would wear off on its own before anyone found out. If not, he'd have to own up to his mother – or far, far worse, to Fay Paradox – and beg for help.

So he pulled the door to, clomped as softly as he could back along the landing, picking up his slippers on the way, climbed into bed and pulled the covers tight round him. His furry legs felt all tickly and uncomfortable between the smooth sheets, as if they would have preferred to be in scratchy straw, but that didn't stop him from drifting off to sleep eventually.

He knew from the tickly feeling that nothing had worn off when he was woken by Fay Paradox's tap on their door next morning.

"The worm won't wait!" she called brightly.

"We've got to be early birds, I suppose she means," said Lorna. "Gosh James, you look a bit funny this morning. It's your ears! Are they always as pointy as that?"

"No!" James almost shrieked, then gabbled, "I mean, yes! It's just that they're usually covered by my hair and we don't usually sleep in the same

78

room so you don't usually see them till my hair's over them, usually."

"I see. And is that the same with those pointy bumps on your forehead? Are those usually hidden by your hair too?"

James absolutely could not stop his hand going up to feel them, and of course Lorna was right – there they were, one each side like little horns. He had a feeling that she knew there was something strange going on, but like a good sister she was helping him to pretend there wasn't. At any rate, she soon got herself dressed and off down to breakfast without asking any more awkward questions.

The moment the door had closed behind her, James leapt out of bed, slipped his pyjamas off and ran to the long mirror on the wardrobe to weigh

up the damage. The main hope in his
mind now was that he could keep it
hidden till Mum got back – he'd a
hundred times rather tell her how
stupid he'd been than tell Fay
Paradox. He was sure Mum would be
able to undo the spell in a couple of
seconds.

Starting at the top . . . luckily his
hair really was quite long. By fluffing it
up and twisting it round a bit, he could
hide all except the very tips of the little
horns, and the tips of his ears were no
problem at all. So far, so good. As for
the rest of him . . . well, the fur from
his waist to his feet would be covered
by his clothes so that only left the feet.
He could see at once that there was no
chance of keeping any shoes on little
hooves like that. Maybe he'd think of
something in a minute.

It wasn't till he was turning away to start putting his clothes on that a new horror caught his eye. A tail! He had a tail – a long, thickish, leathery tail with something like a little arrowhead on the end. It reached almost to the floor.

Getting dressed was therefore not too easy. After a struggle with his tail, because it did seem to have a mind of its own and want to keep waving about, he managed to tuck it uncomfortably down one leg of his jeans. But he hadn't realised how different the shape of his lower half was – far wider hips that he was terrified would burst the jeans open if he could ever get them done up.

It wasn't till he finally had got them zipped up that he realised how much shorter his legs were. He despaired, and was just about to give up when he suddenly saw that it actually answered his main problem. With the bottoms of his jeans rolled up a little, but not too much, his feet were so well hidden that he didn't need to put shoes on at all.

Looking again in the mirror when he'd finished, he had to admit that he still looked odd, especially with no feet, but there was just a faint chance that neither Lorna nor Fay Paradox would notice. Anyway, there wasn't much more to be done about it except clomp downstairs to breakfast.

Fay Paradox laid on such entertainments for them that day that it should have been wonderful. For Lorna, of course, it *was* wonderful, and even James managed to forget his discomforts and fears of being found out for quite a bit of the time.

She took them kite-flying on
Marbury Hill – only being Fay
Paradox's kites, they did extraordinary
things like changing their shapes, and
looping and dancing about together in
the sky of their own accord. Once one
of them even lifted Lorna a little
distance off the ground and sailed her
around for a while before putting her
gently back down.

After lunch Fay Paradox conjured
them a box of Unearthly Delights
chocolates out of the air. They were
even far more gorgeous and dreamy
than James and Lorna had
remembered, because Unearthly
Delights always are. Then, because it
began to rain ("I could do something
about that," Fay Paradox said, "but
we can have fun indoors too"), they
stayed in and drew pictures with

pencils and pens which somehow made their pictures come out much more beautifully than they could ever have hoped.

Occasionally, too, Fay Paradox would touch one of their pictures with her hand and it would come to life. A picnicking family which Lorna drew began passing sandwiches to each other and rolling around on the grass, giggling as picnicking families do.

Two cars which James drew chased each other madly round the paper with brakes and tyres screeching.

And all this time, no one said anything about James's strange lack of feet or his strange hairstyle. It wasn't till they heard the sound of Bill's taxi pulling up at the front of the house that he remembered how he'd still got to face his mum and own up to what he'd done.

Fay Paradox did something rather odd then. As she went to open the front door to let Virbena and Bill in, she passed behind James, and putting one hand on his head, bent down and whispered in his ear, "A leopard – even a nosey leopard – ought to have his own spots, oughtn't he?"

Since James had no idea what she meant he didn't answer, and in any

case he was soon too busy greeting
Mum and Dad to try and work it out.

"We had a *lovely* time," Virbena was
saying, "and I'll bet you had a lovely
time too."

They both nodded furiously.

"But James, really!" Virbena said in
a shocked voice. "What on earth are
you doing going round in bare feet
with your trousers rolled up like that?"

James looked down, and indeed they
were real bare feet poking out of his
jeans there – his own, dear bare feet,
with toes he could wiggle, and no fur
anywhere in sight. He didn't even need
to touch his ears or his forehead to
know that those would be all right
again too.

"I . . . er . . . I'll go and put some
shoes and socks on," was all he could
manage to say.

87

And Fay Paradox simply said, "It takes really an awful lot of curiosity to kill a cat with nine lives, doesn't it?"

Even Amy and Malic, purring welcomingly round Bill and Virbena's legs, seemed to have no answer to that.

Also in Young Puffin

Fanny Witch and the Thunder Lizard

Jeremy Strong

"Oh dear, oh dear. Don't you see? That monster has eaten my Book of Spells. Eaten it!"

Everybody loves Fanny Witch, the schoolteacher, until she magics up a fully grown, live brontosaurus for the children, and the thunder lizard steals her Spell Book so she can't *un*magic the brontosaurus away.

When the boosnatch comes to the village and steals all the children, Fanny Witch has to come to the rescue!